Word List

Here is a list of words that might make it easier to read this book. You'll find them in boldface the first time they appear in the story.

Oslo	OZ-loh
Lillehammer	LIL-lee-ham-er
Norwegian	nor-WEE-juhn
Velkommen	VEL-kum-uhn
God natt	GOH-not
lingonberry	LIN-gon-bair-ee
folktales	FOHK-tayls
coincidence	ko-IN-suh-dens
collapsible	kuh-LAPS-suh-buhl
God dag	GOH-dog
Rena	RAY-nuh
clarinet	KLAIR-uh-net

Barbie™

Mystery at the Snowy Woods Inn

BARBIE and associated trademarks are owned by and used under license from Mattel, Inc. © 1999 Mattel, Inc. All Rights Reserved. Published by Grolier Books, a division of Grolier Enterprises, Inc. Story by Claire Jordan. Photo crew: Paul Jordan, Laura Lynch, Patrick Kittel, Dave Bateman, Steve Alfano, and Lisa Collins. Produced by Bumpy Slide Books. Printed in the United States of America.

ISBN: 0-7172-8889-7

GROLIER
B O O K S

Chapter One

"Hooray, we're almost there!" Judy said brightly. She set her bags down in the train station. She and Barbie had just flown into **Oslo,** the capital city of Norway. Now they would take a train farther north to the town of **Lillehammer.**

Barbie pointed to one of the tracks. "There's our train. We'd better get going."

But before Judy could pick up her suitcase, a large man tripped over it. He tumbled to the ground, his bags clanging loudly as they hit the floor.

"Oh!" exclaimed Judy. "Are you okay?"

The tall man straightened his yellow ski hat

and muttered something in what sounded like
Norwegian.

Barbie bent down to help pick up the bags.
A shorter man shouted at her. He grabbed his
friend's things. Then the two men hurried away.

"It was an accident," Judy called.

"Of course it was," said a voice behind them.

The friends turned to see a red-haired woman
in a pink ski jacket. A long, thin, blue duffel bag
was leaning up against her shoulder. "I saw what
happened," the woman
said. "Those men
were so rude!"

"I guess they had
to hurry to catch the
train to Lillehammer,"
Barbie said. She looked
at her watch. "And so do we!"

"That's my train as well," the woman replied.
Soon the three women had settled into their

seats and were leaving Oslo's busy streets behind.

Barbie looked out the window. The land was more open as they traveled north to Lillehammer. In the distance, she could see cross-country skiers gliding across snow-covered fields.

The red-haired woman introduced herself as Greta. Barbie introduced herself and Judy. She explained that she was a sports reporter for *Snow Scene* magazine. Judy was a photographer. They had come to cover Norway's biggest cross-country ski race, the Birch Legs Race.

Greta gestured toward the skis in the duffel bag at her feet. "I'm entered in the race myself. This year, they have added a special prize. A wealthy man who won the race years ago is giving a bag of rare silver coins to the winner."

"We should get a picture of the prize for our article," Barbie said, writing in her notebook.

"Where will you be staying?" Greta asked.

Judy pulled a piece of paper out of her bag.

"The Snowy Woods Inn," she read out loud.

A strange look came over Greta's face.

Barbie frowned. "Is there a problem?"

Greta sighed. "Perhaps I shouldn't say anything. It's just that the inn has had some problems . . ."

Barbie and Judy looked at each other.

" . . . with elves," Greta finished.

"We're not *that* close to the North Pole, are we?" Judy joked.

Greta laughed. "I know this must sound silly to outsiders. But elves are taken quite seriously here. Many Norwegians believe that certain old houses have elves who live under the floors. They say that at night you can hear their low, sad music. Other elves can be trouble. They break and steal things. And they bring very bad luck."

"Is that the problem with the inn?" asked Judy.

Greta nodded. "People say that years ago, the owner bought twelve silver glasses, or goblets. He didn't have much money. He did it to please the elves and bring good luck to his inn. Elves love silver, you see. Sure enough, his luck improved. But then one of the glasses disappeared. The owner suspected his houseboys and fired them. Business suffered. The inn became run-down. People started calling it the Sorry Woods Inn. The owner blamed the elves. In a fit of anger, he closed the inn, saying the elves could have it. The inn stayed closed for many years. But last year, a young couple bought it and fixed it up. I heard that the goblets came with the place. But the elves must have come with it, too."

Judy's eyes widened. "What do you mean?"

Greta leaned forward and explained. "The new owners have also had troubles: Pipes have burst for no reason. Brand-new appliances haven't worked. The new owners say that these things are normal in an old building. But business hasn't been good. Who would want to stay at the Snowy Woods Inn when it's home to such a bad elf?"

Barbie chuckled halfheartedly. "Us, I guess!"

Chapter Two

When the train pulled into Lillehammer late that afternoon, it was already dark outside. Barbie and Judy said good-bye to Greta and headed for their rental car. "Do you think there's anything to this elf stuff?" Judy asked.

Barbie shrugged. "I guess we'll find out."

It wasn't long before they reached a gravel road that led to the Snowy Woods Inn. Judy looked up from the map. "Turn here," she directed Barbie. The car's headlights cut through the darkness. The tires crunched over the frozen ground. Pine trees towered over them.

Finally they saw the lights of the inn. Barbie parked the car. The two women carried their bags up to the front porch. The old wooden planks creaked under their feet.

Barbie peeked through the window. A warm fire crackled in the lobby fireplace. Wood paneling and simple pine furniture gave the inn a cozy feeling. "It looks nice inside," she reassured Judy. Barbie opened the front door.

"Velkommen!" A man with brown hair and blue eyes greeted them in Norwegian. It was Mr. Nansen, one of the owners.

His wife, Mrs. Nansen, smiled at her guests. "I'm sorry the walkway is so dark. The lights have to be fixed."

Then a blond-haired boy appeared from behind the front desk. "This is our son, Anders," she added.

Barbie and Judy smiled at the couple and shook Anders's small hand. The two women were hungry after their long trip. They happily accepted

their hosts' invitation to dinner. Barbie and Judy took their bags to their rooms. Then they went downstairs to the small dining room. Only a few tables were set up.

While the friends waited for a table, Barbie noticed a wooden cabinet with glass doors. Inside she could see shiny, silver goblets. Each goblet had the same diamond pattern on the side. Barbie counted them, ". . . ten, eleven."

"Hmmm," she thought. "So at least the part in Greta's story about the missing goblet seems to be true."

A small man with light gray hair noticed the women waiting. He stood up and walked over to them. "I am finished. Please, take my table," he said.

Barbie and Judy thanked him and waited as the table was cleared and set.

After signing the bill, the man pulled a silver pocket watch out of his vest. He flipped open the shiny cover.

Barbie could see the initials *E.S.* engraved on it. She noticed that the man had a silver ring and cuff links as well.

"You must like silver very much," Barbie observed. "Are you a collector?"

The man smiled as he put away his watch. "You might say that," he replied. "Excuse me," he added politely, "I must thank my hostess." He walked across the room to say a few words to Mrs. Nansen. Then he left.

"***God natt,*** Mr. Flagstad," said Mrs. Nansen, waving good night to the elderly gentleman.

Barbie and Judy sat down at the table near the window. Mrs. Nansen came over to take their order. "May I recommend the meat cakes and potato dumplings?" she asked. "Perhaps with pickled herring and **lingonberry** jam?"

The two women thought that sounded

11

delicious. As Mrs. Nansen walked away, Judy whispered, "Barbie, there's something moving behind that tablecloth."

Barbie turned to see a small figure hiding behind the table. Then she realized the figure was wearing little sneakers! "Anders?" she called softly. The little boy shyly peered out from behind the tablecloth. He tiptoed over to their table and explained, "I'm hiding from the elf."

"What elf?" Judy asked, grinning.

"Mr. Flagstad. He's an elf in disguise," the boy declared.

Barbie smiled. "What makes you think that?"

"Did you see his silver hair?" Anders replied. "And his silver watch? And his silver ring? He even wears a silver coat! Only elves have that much silver. And he's small like an elf, too. I want to get a picture of him to show my friend Magnus at school."

While Anders was speaking, his mother

returned with two steaming plates. "Run along," Mrs. Nansen said to the eight-year-old. "I'm sorry," she told Barbie and Judy. "Anders hears many stories about elves. Our country's **folktales** are full of them. Anders likes to think they are real."

After dinner, the women thanked Mrs. Nansen for a delicious meal. "Do you know where the prize for the ski race is being kept?" Judy asked her. "I'd like to photograph those coins tomorrow."

"They're at the bank," Mrs. Nansen informed them. "I wish I could win the prize myself. Then maybe we could afford . . ." The innkeeper stopped, embarrassed. "Would you like anything else?" she asked, changing the subject.

Barbie and Judy thanked her and said that they didn't. Then Mrs. Nansen excused herself.

Judy suggested they get some pictures of downtown Lillehammer at night. Barbie agreed.

While Judy ran upstairs to get her camera, Barbie waited in the lobby. When Judy returned, she asked, "Would you mind if I take a few shots of you to check if my flash is working?"

"Not at all," Barbie replied. She stood near the front door and smiled. Just as Judy started snapping, the door behind Barbie opened. Two men stepped in. One was wearing a yellow ski hat, the other a red scarf. They both looked upset.

Barbie turned around and recognized them. "Hello," she said. "We bumped into you at the train station, remember?"

The shorter man looked at Barbie. He said something in Norwegian to his friend. Then both men smiled and nodded. "I'm Thor," said the shorter man. "This is my friend, Olaf."

Barbie and Judy introduced themselves. Then Judy commented, "It's quite a **coincidence** that we're staying at the same inn. Especially one out in the middle of the woods." Then she added, "You must be here for the big race."

Olaf nodded. "We'll be skiing in it."

"But where are your skis? I don't recall seeing them at the train station," she said.

"Oh, er, uh," Olaf stammered.

Then Thor whispered, "We're going to use new **collapsible** skis that fold up."

"Really?" Barbie asked. She pulled out her notepad and pen and started writing. "I've never heard of collapsible skis. Could you tell me more about them? Judy and I work for a sports magazine. This would make a great article."

"We invented them," Olaf said proudly. "Nobody else in the world has them."

Thor added quickly, "We will use the skis in the race this Saturday. Until then, we want to keep them a secret." He smiled at Barbie. "I'm sure you understand?"

Barbie closed her notepad. "Of course," she replied. "Then may I interview you after the race?"

Olaf looked at Thor. "Certainly," Thor agreed. "Excuse us. We must be going."

"We'll see you later," Barbie said, waving. When they were gone, she said to Judy, "Ready?"

Judy shook her head. "No. This flash needs to recharge more. I'll get my backup camera and be right down." Judy went back to her room and returned a few minutes later.

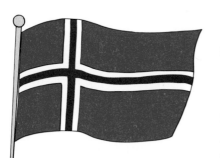

The two women decided to drive downtown. The restaurants and shops were crowded. Barbie and Judy saw flags and banners near the stadium where the race would end.

"I'll have to remember that for tomorrow," Judy said with a yawn.

It was nine o'clock when they finally returned to the inn. They both were exhausted. Barbie had just sat down when she heard a loud knock on her door. When she opened the door, Judy rushed inside.

"My camera!" Judy cried. "It's gone!"

Chapter Three

The two friends rushed back to Judy's room. "I left it on the dresser!" Judy explained. "I'm sure I locked my door before we left. But when we came back, it was unlocked."

They searched everywhere, but the camera was gone. Nothing else was missing. Barbie phoned the front desk. In seconds, Mr. and Mrs. Nansen were in Judy's room. Anders was right behind them. "I know who took your camera," the boy said proudly.

Mr. Nansen looked down at his son. "If you do, you had better tell us," he said sternly.

18

"The elf!" Anders blurted out.

"Now, that's enough!" his mother scolded. "I don't want to hear any more of that foolishness!"

The little boy looked embarrassed.

Mr. Nansen looked around. "Nothing else was taken?" he asked.

"No. That's the odd thing," Judy replied.

The Nansens seemed upset. But to Barbie's surprise, they didn't want to call the police. "We will find your camera ourselves," Mrs. Nansen promised. "We're sorry about this." They took Anders by the hand and said good night.

"I'm sure it will turn up," Barbie reassured Judy. "With any luck, Anders's 'elf' might decide to return it!" she joked.

"Very funny," Judy sighed.

That night, Barbie dreamt that small figures were moving through the dining room. They were in Judy's room. They were under Barbie's bed. They were playing music—low, sad music. Barbie

19

sat up in bed with a start. She wasn't dreaming. She *did* hear music!

It was coming from outside. Barbie rushed to the window and peered into the blackness. She could see a light shining in the dark woods behind the inn. She also saw a small, silver figure moving toward the inn. Barbie's heart pounded as she raced to Judy's room. She banged on the door. When Judy opened it, Barbie pulled her to the window.

"I don't see anything," Judy mumbled, covering a yawn.

Barbie stared into the night. The light and the figure were gone. "I was sure I saw something," she said, rubbing her eyes. "I know I heard music. I thought it was a dream, but then . . ." She sighed.

"Maybe you've heard too many elf stories," Judy told her friend.

"Maybe," Barbie replied, half smiling. "I'll see you in the morning." Then she headed back to her own room.

After breakfast the next morning, Barbie
and Judy ran into Mrs. Nansen in the lobby with
Anders. She was zipping up his coat and kissing
him good-bye. She turned to her two guests and
said, "Do you still want to see the coins at the
bank? Anders can show you the shortcut through
the woods. He goes to school that way."

Judy looked at Barbie and nodded. "We'd
like that," Barbie replied.

"I've drawn you a map to help you find
your way back,"
Mrs. Nansen said.
She handed them
a piece of paper,
and they turned
to leave.

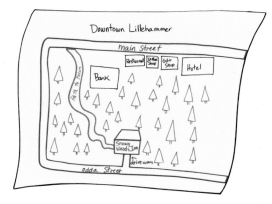

Suddenly
Mrs. Nansen called, "Look out!"

Barbie turned just in time to avoid tripping

over a mop and bucket. The floor of the lobby was covered with muddy footprints. Barbie paused and stared at the dirty floor.

"Somebody forgot to wipe his feet," Judy noted, shaking her head.

Barbie and Judy put on their gloves and hats and zipped up their jackets. Anders was waiting outside. "Did you hear the elf music last night?" he asked them. "I can't wait to tell Magnus."

So it wasn't a dream! "Elf music!" Barbie exclaimed.

Anders nodded and began walking. "It sounded sad," he told them, "but I'm glad it was their sad music and not their happy music. Magnus says that if you hear their happy music, it makes you dance and dance until you can't dance anymore!"

They followed Anders around to the back of the inn. The young boy ran ahead of them and disappeared among the thick trees.

"So you *did* hear something," Judy said slowly.

Barbie's eyes searched the dark woods. Even in daylight, they were eerie.

Up ahead, the women could see the boy's small figure skipping down the snow-covered path. They hurried to catch up with him. It wasn't long before they found themselves behind a building. They wanted to ask Anders where they were. But when they looked around, the boy was gone.

Barbie shrugged and said, "The way he appears and disappears, *he* could be an elf!"

Judy nodded and looked at the map. "This must be the bank," she declared.

"Then we had better get to work," Barbie replied. As they walked around the building, the frozen ground crunched under their boots. Barbie looked back at the dark woods behind her.

Chapter Four

The bank wasn't open yet, so Barbie
and Judy decided to walk into downtown
Lillehammer. Racers were everywhere. Barbie
was pulling her notepad out of her bag when a
familiar voice called, ***"God dag."***

The women looked up to see Greta, the
racer they had met on the train. "Good morning,"
they replied. Greta was happy to see them again.
And she didn't mind being interviewed for their
magazine.

Barbie took out her tape recorder. "I hear
that racers wear small packs during the race. Is

that true?" she asked.

"Yes," the Norwegian woman replied. "About eight hundred years ago, two people skied from Lillehammer to the town of **Rena** carrying the king of Norway."

"A Norwegian who didn't ski?" Judy joked.

Greta smiled. "The king was only a baby at the time. The skiers saved him from his enemies. The Birch Legs Race is held in honor of that difficult journey. Today, skiers carry eight-pound packs as a symbol of the king's weight. To protect themselves from the cold, the original skiers wore bark from birch trees on their legs. That is how the race

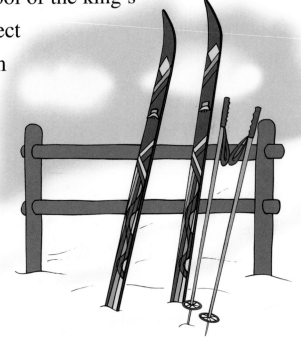

got its name.

"Nowadays the Birch Legs Race begins in Rena," Greta told them. "But most people stay in Lillehammer. Shuttle buses take the skiers to Rena on race day."

When the interview was over, Barbie thanked Greta. Then she interviewed other racers while Judy took photos. When they were finished, the two friends went back to the bank to see the silver coins.

They spoke to the bank manager, who led them to a glass case in the lobby. Inside, shiny silver coins spilled out of a cloth sack.

"This will make a great picture!" Judy told him. She took shots from different angles.

"It will make a great story, too!" Barbie added. She asked the manager some questions about the rare coins. "Aren't you worried about the coins being stolen?"

"No," the bank manager told her. "We

have an alarm system." He waved to a nearby staircase. "At night, we put the coins downstairs in the safe."

Just as Judy was finishing up, Barbie saw Thor and Olaf enter the bank. When he noticed Barbie, Olaf tripped on the top step. Thor grabbed the taller man's arm to keep him from falling.

"Hello," Barbie called. She and Judy walked over to the two men. "We seem to keep running into each other. What are you doing here?"

Barbie thought she saw a startled look pass over Thor's face. But it quickly changed into a smile. He leaned over and whispered, "We decided to keep our collapsible skis in the bank's safe. They're in a safe-deposit box. After all, if someone could steal your camera, they could steal our invention, too."

"It's a strong safe," Olaf added. "We—"

"—have to go," Thor finished. They quickly said good-bye and hurried downstairs.

Barbie thought for a moment. Something didn't make sense. "Those skis must fold up pretty small to fit inside a safe-deposit box," she commented.

The two women left the bank. They set off on the path through the woods. But something was bothering Barbie. Finally she said, "Judy, did you tell Thor about your camera being stolen?"

Before Judy could answer, a small figure leapt out from behind a tree. Startled, the two women jumped back.

"Anders!" Judy scolded the laughing boy. "It's not nice to scare people like that!"

The boy looked at his feet. "I'm sorry," he said. "I was just playing in the woods on my way home from school. And I found something. Come see! Please!" he begged.

Barbie and Judy agreed and followed the boy into the woods. They had to push aside twigs and branches to clear a path for themselves. Soon

Anders stopped beside a large tree. "Look!" he told them, pointing to the ground.

Barbie crouched down. The snow had been cleared away from the base of the tree. The frozen ground had been overturned. A mound of dark-brown soil lay on top of the white snow.

"It's an elf tunnel," Anders declared.

Then Barbie noticed something. A design had been carved into the tree trunk. It was so faint that she could barely make it out. It looked as if it had been carved many years ago. It reminded her of the diamond pattern on the goblets. She pushed aside the cold soil. As she did, Barbie's fingers touched a small, thin piece of wood. She picked it up.

Judy peered at it. "It's a reed from the mouthpiece of a **clarinet**!" she declared. "I used to play clarinet in my high school band."

Barbie was puzzled. "But how did it get here?" she asked.

The boy spoke up. "It belongs to the elf. Remember the music we heard last night?"

Barbie did remember. Maybe someone *had* been playing music in the woods last night. But who? And why? Barbie quietly tucked the wooden reed into her pocket.

As they headed back to the inn, Anders confessed, "Our house elf has been taking things lately."

"Really?" Barbie replied. "Like what?"

"Oh," Anders shrugged, "this and that. This morning, Papa couldn't find his red shovel. And when he did, the handle was broken. Mama told me not to tell anybody because it makes our inn look bad. But you and Judy aren't afraid of our elf, are you?"

Barbie and Judy looked at each other. "No,

we're not," Judy replied.

Finally they arrived at the inn. They said good-bye to Anders as he ran inside.

Barbie and Judy stood on the front porch. Barbie flipped open her notepad and started writing. Someone—or some*thing*—had been digging in those woods. It would take a strong person to dig in the frozen ground. Could it be related to the broken shovel? Why were the Nansens being so secretive about Judy's camera? What else were they trying to hide? Barbie felt the reed in her pocket. And what about that late-night clarinet player? "Something strange is going on here," she told Judy. "And I'm going to find out what it is."

Chapter Five

When Barbie and Judy entered the inn, they saw Mrs. Nansen handing skis to Thor and Olaf.

"We'll use these for practice," Thor explained.

Mrs. Nansen watched them leave. "I am surprised they didn't bring their own skis," she said.

Barbie caught Judy's eye. They had agreed to keep the collapsible skis a secret. Then they headed upstairs to Barbie's room to try to make sense of the strange events.

"Let's see," Barbie began. "We've got a light in the woods."

"And a hole by a tree," Judy continued. "A

missing camera and strange music . . ."

Then a thought occurred to Barbie. "Judy, you know that little man staying here? Isn't it strange that his watch has the initials *E.S.* on it even though his name is Flagstad?"

"Maybe it stands for *Elf's Silver!*" Judy said with a wink.

Barbie laughed and threw a pillow at her. "My head is swimming! Why don't we try out one of the ski trails to clear our minds?"

"Great idea," Judy agreed.

Barbie and Judy each borrowed a pair of cross-country skis from the inn. "I'm sorry they aren't new," Mrs. Nansen apologized. She sighed, then brightened. "But there is a wonderful trail that runs near the lake. I will give you directions. I just sent some of our other guests there."

After a short walk, Barbie and Judy arrived at the lake and put on their skis. Soon they were gliding along the peaceful trail. The branches of the trees hung low with the weight of the heavy snow.

After a while, Barbie and Judy came upon two other skiers on the trail. One of them seemed to be having trouble. When Barbie got closer, she realized the skiers were Thor and Olaf. Thor was gliding along smoothly. But poor Olaf was skidding and stumbling from side to side. Frustrated, Thor was shouting at him in Norwegian. Barbie and Judy skied up to them.

"His big feet," Thor explained to Barbie, "that's the problem!"

Olaf lurched over. "No, it's these old skis!" he protested. "Why doesn't that inn have new skis?"

"They will soon," said a voice behind them. Everyone turned to see Mr. Flagstad making his way over to them in a pair of snowshoes. "I guess the Nansens recommend this trail to all their guests," he said. Then he turned to Olaf. "Would you mind if I gave you some pointers?" he asked politely.

The large man gave him a smile and replied, "Not at all!"

The older man showed Olaf how to balance his movement on the skis. Olaf seemed to catch on quickly.

"Do you give ski lessons?" Judy asked the older gentleman.

Mr. Flagstad shook his head. "No, but I used to ski. Now I just snowshoe."

"You said that the inn would have new

skis soon," commented Barbie.

Mr. Flagstad smiled. "The Nansens will have many new things soon," he informed Barbie. "Their luck is about to change. I am sure of it." The gentleman touched his hat and said, "*God dag.*" And he disappeared into the woods.

Barbie thought it was strange that Olaf was such a poor skier. He and Thor were entered in

the race! The women skied a bit more and headed back to the inn. It was starting to snow lightly. They ate dinner and went upstairs to their rooms.

Later that night, Barbie couldn't sleep. Her mind was too full of questions. "I might as well begin typing up my interviews," she thought as she got out of bed. She had just plugged in her laptop computer when there was a knock on the door.

Barbie opened it, and Judy rushed in. She pulled Barbie to the window. It had stopped snowing. A light was moving through the trees! They were about to run downstairs when it disappeared.

"We're too late! Let's get up early tomorrow and look for footprints," Barbie suggested. "With the fresh cover of snow, whoever—or *what*ever— is out there has probably left tracks."

Chapter Six

Early the next morning, Barbie and Judy
hurried through the woods, searching for footprints.
They arrived at the tree marked with the diamond.
But when Barbie looked down, she saw that the
hole had been filled up. The ground around the
tree was brushed smooth. Somebody was trying
to cover up something.

"Someone *was* here," Judy said. "But wasn't
the light coming from over there?" she asked,
pointing in the other direction.

"I think so," Barbie agreed. So they headed
back toward the path. Just then, Barbie pointed

down. "Fresh footprints! And they're too big to be an elf's!" she added.

The two women followed the large footprints through the woods to the back wall of the bank. There they discovered a small mound of dirt against the wall. Barbie moved the dirt aside with her boot and discovered a hole. From it, she could see a thick wire running up the wall and into the bank. Barbie looked down at the freshly turned soil. She remembered the muddy footprints Mrs. Nansen had been cleaning up the day before.

"I think," Barbie said slowly, "that elves aren't the only ones who like silver."

"What do you mean?" asked Judy.

"Let's just say that this is finally starting to make some sense," Barbie told her. "Come on!"

The two women hurried around the building. They met the bank manager on his way in. Barbie asked the bank manager about the wire in the back. He looked at her curiously. "That's the wire to the alarm," he said. "What made you notice it?"

"Someone else may have noticed it before me," Barbie explained. "Are the coins going to be moved to the finish line for tomorrow's race?"

The bank manager nodded. "We'll take them out of the safe at noon tomorrow."

"The safe?" Barbie asked. "So they won't be on display tomorrow?"

"Oh, no," said the manager. "Tomorrow is Saturday. The bank will be closed to customers."

Barbie thought about what he had said. Then she asked the bank manager for a favor. "Would you please call me if anyone comes to remove anything from the safe-deposit boxes today?"

"I guess I could do that," he agreed, "but why?"

Barbie smiled knowingly. "Because I believe those silver coins are in danger of being stolen. And if Judy and I hurry, we might be able to stop the thieves in time!"

Back at the hotel, Barbie asked Mrs. Nansen if she had seen Thor and Olaf.

"No," Mrs. Nansen replied. "They said they would be practicing all day. They made reservations for the first bus to Rena tomorrow morning."

Barbie nodded. "Mrs. Nansen, I don't mean to be nosy, but do you know anything about Mr. Flagstad?"

"Not really," she replied. "He just checked in a few days ago. He loves to ski, but he can't any longer. He seems to like the inn very much."

Barbie and Judy went back to Barbie's room. The two women made their plan carefully. Then they called the bank manager. No one had taken anything out of the safe-deposit boxes all day.

"It's time to put our plan into action," Barbie declared. "Let's go to the police." Then the two women hurried downtown with all of their notes.

Chapter Seven

The next morning, Barbie and Judy sat in the dining room of the Snowy Woods Inn. Barbie looked out the window at the falling snow. The police had just left with the thieves.

Mr. Nansen shook his head and sat down. "But how did you know the silver coins were in danger?" he asked.

"We saw that someone had been digging around the alarm wire at the bank," Judy said. "The rare coins were going to be moved the next day. So it made sense that thieves were after them."

Mrs. Nansen shook her head and shivered.

"It's frightening to think that our guests could be bank robbers. But how," she wondered, "did you know it was Thor and Olaf?"

"Do you remember the large, muddy footprints you cleaned up the other day?" Barbie asked her hostess.

"Of course," Mrs. Nansen replied. "The floors don't usually get that muddy until spring."

"Exactly!" Barbie stated. "This time of year, the ground is covered with snow. So the only way to make *muddy* footprints is to step in freshly dug dirt. And the footprints we saw in the snow around the bank were as large as the ones in the lobby."

Judy continued. "Thor and Olaf stayed here because of your location. They used the shortcut through the woods to sneak to the bank at night and dig the hole. The light we saw in the woods the other night was probably them. They must have been coming back from the bank."

"*They* must have borrowed my shovel," Mr.

Nansen said, thinking out loud.

Barbie nodded. "The thieves planned to escape by posing as racers," she explained. "They would carry the coins in their packs. Since all the other racers would be carrying packs, they could blend into the crowd. Thor and Olaf planned to take the first shuttle bus to Rena. They would be gone before anyone noticed the coins were missing."

Barbie continued, "But we weren't sure until last night, when the bank closed. Thor had told us they were storing collapsible skis in a safe-deposit box at the bank. We knew that if they were telling the truth, they would have had to get their skis out yesterday. The bank would be closed today—race day. When the bank manager said that no one had taken anything out of the safe on Friday, we knew they had made up the whole story."

"The police said that Thor's an alarm specialist," Judy explained. "He and Olaf visited the safe-deposit boxes at the bank. They needed to see the setup of the bank's safe."

"And that's where they hid Judy's camera," said Barbie. "They didn't want to get caught with it here at the inn."

Judy patted the camera next to her. "The police found it and returned it to me," she added.

Anders had been quiet the whole time. But now he asked, "So the elf didn't take your camera?"

Everyone laughed. "No, it was Olaf," Judy told the boy. "He thought that I had taken a picture of him and Thor. So he broke into my room and stole the camera."

"That was another clue," Barbie said. She turned to the Nansens. "You had wanted to keep the missing camera a secret. But Thor and Olaf somehow knew about it, even though none of us had mentioned it to them."

Mr. Nansen looked down. "I'm sorry," he apologized. "I would have called the police about the camera. It's just that we've been having such bad luck lately. I was afraid more tales about elves would hurt our business."

"There are some things I still don't understand," Judy said, turning to Barbie. "If Olaf was digging by the bank, who was digging by Anders's tree? What about the silver figure in the woods? And that strange music?"

"It *was* an elf!" Anders burst out. "And there he is!"

Everyone turned toward the doorway.

"I'm afraid I'm not your elf," Mr. Flagstad said, walking over to the table.

"Oh, I must apologize for my son!" Mrs. Nansen told her guest.

"No, Mrs. Nansen," he corrected. "It is I who should apologize. I believe this belongs to you," he said. He handed her a beautiful silver goblet with a diamond pattern on the side.

Everyone at the table gasped. "It's the missing silver goblet!" Mrs. Nansen exclaimed. "But where did you find it after all these years?"

"In the woods," Mr. Flagstad began, taking off his silver coat and sitting down. "But let me explain. Fifty years ago, I worked at this inn with another houseboy. We worked very hard. But the owner didn't pay us much. Instead, he bought a set of goblets for the inn.

"One night, on my way home, I saw the other houseboy going into the woods. I was curious, so I followed. I saw him digging by the base of a small tree. After he had left, I looked at the tree. A diamond pattern had been carved into the trunk. The next day, the owner accused us of stealing one of his silver goblets. He fired us both. I was sure that the missing goblet was buried by the tree. But I was so angry that I just left. On my way home, I noticed a shiny object on the ground. I brushed aside some leaves and found a silver coin. I picked it up and put it in my pocket.

"Then, that very year, I entered the Birch Legs race and won. Soon after, I got a job with a silversmith. I learned all I could. Eventually I opened my own shop. Things went very well." He paused. "You may call this superstition, but I thought that the silver coin had brought me luck. Perhaps the elf felt sorry for me and had left it for me to find," he said with a twinkle in his eye.

The man continued, "Soon afterward, the innkeeper's luck did change for the worse, and the inn closed. I hadn't thought about the inn for many years when I heard that it had reopened. Then I wanted to search for the goblet and return it to the inn."

Barbie looked at the man's silver coat, draped over the back of his chair. "So *you* were the silver figure we saw in the woods the other night!"

"Yes," he replied. "I was looking for the tree with the diamond pattern. But the ground was too hard for me to dig. So I had to use an ice pick. I worked for two nights and finally dug up the goblet. I guess the other houseboy never came back for it. He must have been ashamed of what he had done." He looked at the goblet and then at Mrs. Nansen. "I hope it will finally bring you good luck."

The Nansens thanked the elderly man.

"Sir," Barbie said politely, "pardon me, but is Flagstad your real name?"

"No," he admitted. "My real name's Eric Slov."

Mr. Nansen broke in. "*You're* the person who is giving the silver coins for the race prize?"

The man nodded. "That's right. I wanted to bring luck to someone the way one silver coin brought luck to me so many years ago." He thought for a moment and said, "With your permission, Mr. and Mrs. Nansen, I'd like to present the prize to the winner here at the inn, right after the race."

Mrs. Nansen clasped her hands together.

"That sounds like a wonderful idea!" she cried.

"Yes. All the publicity will be good for business," added her husband excitedly.

Judy looked at her watch and gasped. "That reminds me. Barbie and I have a ski race to cover!"

"Yes, indeed!" Barbie said, standing up. "But I think I have an even more important story to write when we return." She looked at the Nansens. "Mystery at the Snowy Woods Inn."

Then Barbie remembered the small, thin piece of wood in her pocket. "Oh, I almost forgot." She handed Mr. Slov the clarinet reed and said, "I believe this must be yours, Mr. Slov."

The elderly gentleman stared at it and shook his head. "Why, no. I don't play any instruments."

Barbie wondered, "Then who was playing that strange music the other night?"

Anders just smiled at the bigger people's puzzled looks. This was one mystery that only little people knew the answer to.